FIVE
FAVOURITE
NURSERY
TALES

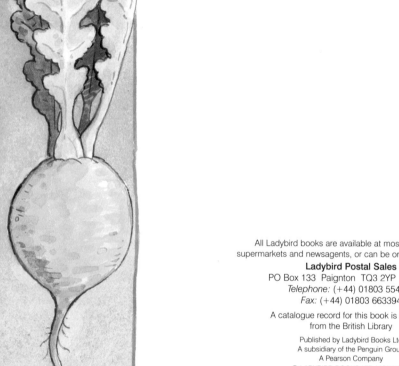

All Ladybird books are available at most bookshops,
supermarkets and newsagents, or can be ordered direct from:
Ladybird Postal Sales
PO Box 133 Paignton TQ3 2YP England
Telephone: (+44) 01803 554761
Fax: (+44) 01803 663394

A catalogue record for this book is available
from the British Library

Published by Ladybird Books Ltd
A subsidiary of the Penguin Group
A Pearson Company
© LADYBIRD BOOKS LTD MCMXCVIII

Stories in this book were previously published by Ladybird Books Ltd
in the *Favourite Tales* series.

LADYBIRD and the device of a Ladybird are trademarks of
Ladybird Books Ltd Loughborough Leicestershire UK

FIVE
FAVOURITE
NURSERY
TALES

Ladybird

Introduction

Children will treasure this collection of timeless nursery tales. The easy-to-read retellings, enhanced by exciting, richly colourful illustrations, faithfully capture all the magic of the original stories.

Contents

The Gingerbread Man

Based on a traditional folk tale
retold by Audrey Daly
Illustrated by Peter Stevenson

Goldilocks and the Three Bears

Based on a traditional folk tale
retold by Audrey Daly
Illustrated by Chris Russell

The Enormous Turnip

Based on a traditional folk tale
retold by Nicola Baxter
Illustrated by Peter Stevenson

The Three Billy Goats Gruff

Based on a traditional folk tale
retold by Joan Stimson
Illustrated by Chris Russell

The Little Red Hen

Based on a traditional folk tale
retold by Ronne Randall
Illustrated by Stephen Holmes

Cover and Borders illustrated by
Peter Stevenson

The Gingerbread Man

Once upon a time, a little old woman and a little old man lived by themselves in a little old house by the side of a road.

One day, the little old woman decided to make a special treat. "I will make a gingerbread man," she said.

So the little old woman made a gingerbread man and put him in the oven to bake. But before long, she heard a tiny voice calling, "Let me out! Let me out!"

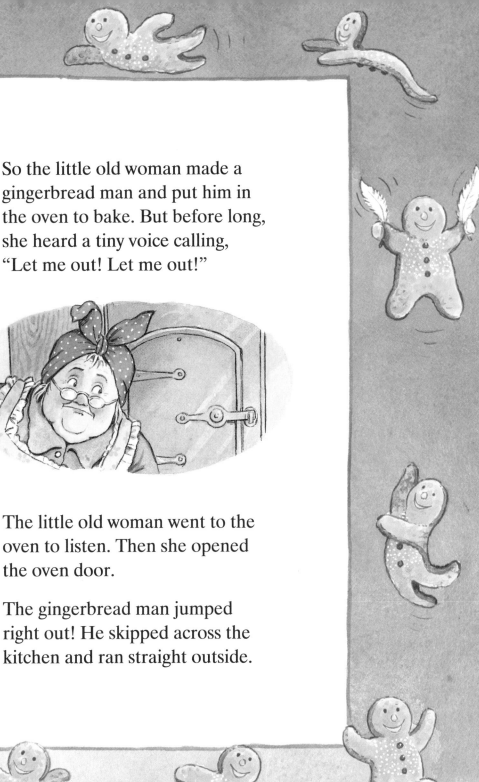

The little old woman went to the oven to listen. Then she opened the oven door.

The gingerbread man jumped right out! He skipped across the kitchen and ran straight outside.

The little gingerbread man was on his way down the road before the little old woman and the little old man were out of the house. They couldn't run nearly as fast as he could.

"Stop! We want to eat you. Stop, little gingerbread man!" they cried, quite out of breath.

But the gingerbread man just sang,

"Run, run, as fast as you can,
You can't catch me,
I'm the gingerbread man!"

Soon the gingerbread man met a cow. "Stop, little man!" mooed the cow. "You look very good to eat!"

But the gingerbread man just ran faster. And he sang,

> *"Run, run, as fast as you can,*
> *You can't catch me,*
> *I'm the gingerbread man!"*

The cow ran and ran, but she could not catch the little gingerbread man.

Farther down the road, the gingerbread man met a horse. "Stop, little man!" said the horse. "You look *very* good to eat, and I'm hungry!"

But the gingerbread man just ran faster.

The horse galloped and galloped as fast as he could, but he wasn't fast enough to catch the gingerbread man.

"I have run away from a little old woman, a little old man, and a cow," cried the gingerbread man. And he sang as he ran,

> "Run, run, as fast as you can,
> You can't catch me,
> I'm the gingerbread man!"

The little gingerbread man ran on and on, going faster and faster. He was very proud of his running, and quite pleased with himself.

At last he met a sly old fox. "Stop! Stop, little man," said the fox, grinning and licking his lips. "I want to talk to you."

But the gingerbread man didn't
stop to listen. He just sang,

"Run, run, as fast as you can,
You can't catch me,
I'm the gingerbread man!"

The cunning old fox could run
very fast indeed, and he ran after
the gingerbread man. He followed
him all the way down the path
through the forest.

Before too long they came to a river. The gingerbread man didn't know what to do.

The cunning old fox wasn't far away. "I'll help you," he said, smiling to himself. "If you jump onto my tail, I will take you across. You will be quite safe and dry."

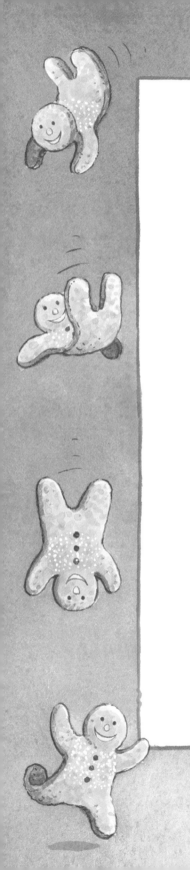

So the little gingerbread man jumped onto the fox's tail and the fox began to swim across the river.

Very soon the fox said, "You are too heavy for my tail. Jump onto my back."

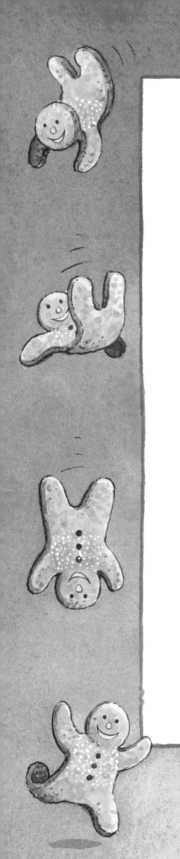

The little gingerbread man
jumped onto the fox's back.

Very soon the fox said, "Little
gingerbread man, you are too
heavy for my back. Why don't you
jump onto my nose?"

And the little gingerbread man jumped onto the fox's nose.

Finally they reached the other side of the river. The fox threw back his head and tossed the gingerbread man high in the air.

Then *down* fell the gingerbread man, and *snap!* went the old fox.

And that was the end of the little gingerbread man.

Goldilocks
and the
Three Bears

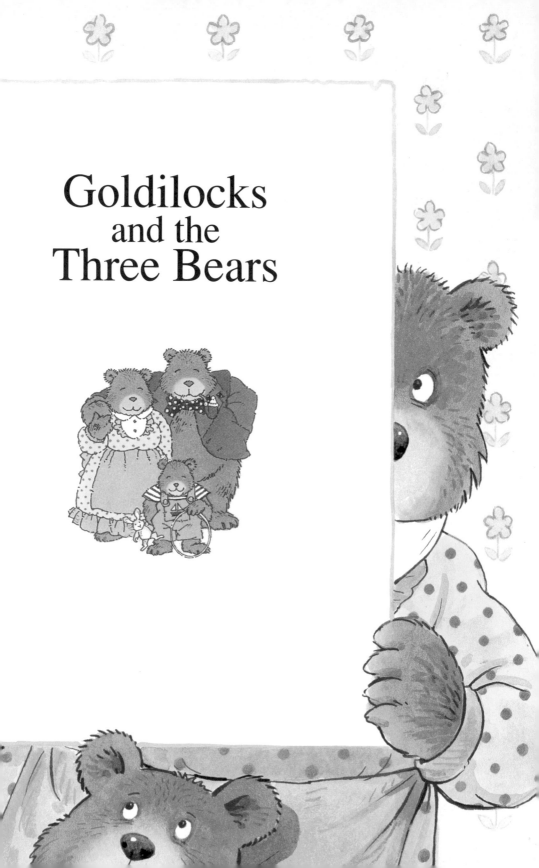

Once upon a time, there were three bears who lived in a little house right in the middle of the forest.

There was great big Father Bear, and medium-sized Mother Bear, and little tiny Baby Bear.

Honey

One morning, Mother Bear made a big pot of porridge and put it into three bowls for breakfast.

But the porridge was much too hot to eat.

"We will leave it to cool while we go for our early morning walk," said Father Bear. "When we come back, it will be just right." So off they went into the forest.

Nearby there lived a very naughty, mischievous little girl. She was called Goldilocks because she had long, golden hair.

That morning, as she was passing the three bears' house, Goldilocks saw that the front door was open.

"I'll just have a little peep inside," she said to herself.

As soon as she saw the porridge, naughty Goldilocks rushed over to taste it. "I do feel rather hungry," she said.

But the porridge in Father Bear's big bowl was still too hot. And the porridge in Mother Bear's medium-sized bowl was lumpy.

At last Goldilocks tried Baby Bear's porridge. It was just right, so she ate up every spoonful!

After that, Goldilocks decided
that she would like to sit down.
But Father Bear's big chair was
much too high.

Next she sat in Mother Bear's medium-sized chair. "This one is much too hard!" she grumbled.

At last she found Baby Bear's tiny chair. It wasn't too high. It wasn't too hard. It was just right!

Goldilocks leaned back happily in Baby Bear's chair. But she was far too heavy. With a *creak* and a *crack*, the chair fell to pieces.

Bump! Goldilocks landed in a heap on the floor. "Well, really!" she said crossly. "I've had such a shock, I shall have to lie down."

So Goldilocks went upstairs. She tried Father Bear's big bed, but that was far too hard.

And Mother Bear's medium-sized bed was far too soft!

"Now this *is* comfortable," sighed Goldilocks, settling into Baby Bear's little bed. And she fell fast asleep!

Before long, the three bears arrived home from their walk.

"I'm ready for my breakfast *right now*," said Father Bear. But when he got to the table he cried out in surprise, "Someone's been eating my porridge!"

"And someone's been eating *my* porridge," said Mother Bear. "I wonder why they didn't like it?"

"They must have liked mine!" cried Baby Bear, holding his empty bowl. "Someone's been eating my porridge, and they've eaten it all up!"

"Look!" said Father Bear. "Someone's been sitting in my chair!"

"And someone's been sitting in *my* chair," said Mother Bear.

"Someone's been sitting in my chair," sobbed poor little Baby Bear, "and they've broken it to pieces!"

The three bears began to search the house. Upstairs, Father Bear looked around. "Someone's been sleeping in my bed!" he said.

"And someone's been sleeping in *my* bed," cried Mother Bear.

"Oh!" squeaked Baby Bear. "Someone's been sleeping in my bed and she's *still here!*"

At the sound of Baby Bear's voice, Goldilocks woke up. The first thing she saw was Father Bear, looking very cross.

Goldilocks jumped up in fright.
She ran down the stairs and out of
the house as fast as she could.

"I don't think she'll trouble us
again," said Father Bear, smiling.

And she never did.

The Enormous Turnip

One sunny morning a man
decided to plant some turnip
seeds.

He fetched his fork from the shed
and dug a patch of his vegetable
garden. It was hard work! He
made sure that there were no
weeds or big stones.

Then, very carefully, he sprinkled
the tiny turnip seeds in a row.

The man took great care of his turnip seeds. Every day, as soon as he woke up, he went down to his vegetable garden and gave them some water.

In only a few days, little green leaves started to appear.

"These are going to be fine turnips," the man said to himself.

The turnips grew very quickly, as turnips do. But one turnip grew faster than all the rest.

Soon it was twice as big as the other turnips. The man was astonished.

"I can almost *see* it growing!" he said proudly.

But the turnip didn't stop. It grew bigger and bigger and bigger until it was… *ENORMOUS!*

One day the man decided that it was time to pull up the enormous turnip.

"We can have it for our dinner," he said to his wife. "I'm sure it will taste as good as it looks!"

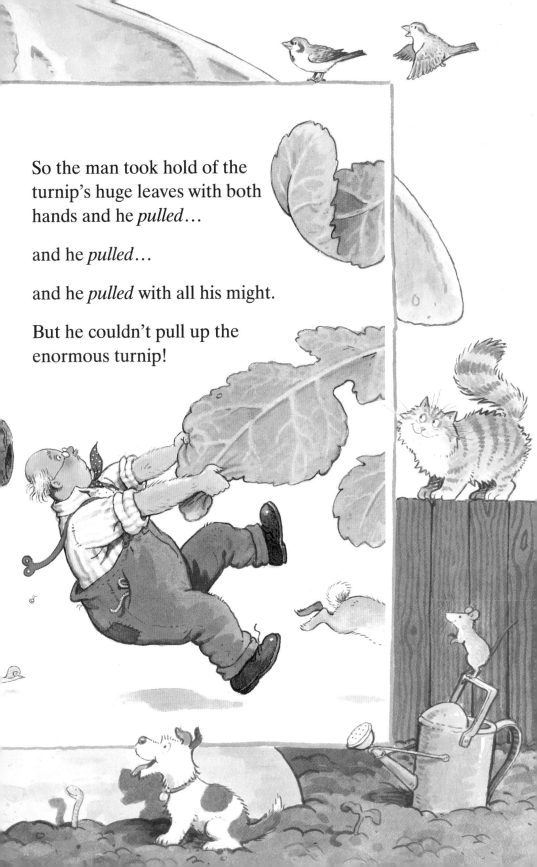

So the man took hold of the turnip's huge leaves with both hands and he *pulled*…

and he *pulled*…

and he *pulled* with all his might.

But he couldn't pull up the enormous turnip!

The man called to his wife. "I'm going to need some help with this turnip!" he laughed.

So the man *pulled* the turnip and the woman *pulled* the man. They *pulled* with all their might.

But they couldn't pull up the enormous turnip!

The woman called to a little boy.
"Can you come and help us with
this enormous turnip?"

So the man *pulled* the turnip and
the woman *pulled* the man and
the little boy *pulled* the woman.
They *pulled* with all their might.

But they couldn't pull up the
enormous turnip!

A little girl was walking past. "Please come and help us with this enormous turnip!" called the little boy.

So the man *pulled* the turnip and the woman *pulled* the man and the little boy *pulled* the woman and the little girl *pulled* the little boy. They *pulled* with all their might.

But they couldn't pull up the enormous turnip!

The little girl called to her dog. "Here boy! Come and help us!"

So the man *pulled* the turnip and the woman *pulled* the man and the little boy *pulled* the woman and the little girl *pulled* the little boy and the dog *pulled* the little girl. They *pulled* with all their might.

But they couldn't pull up the enormous turnip!

The dog saw a large orange cat walking along the fence. "Woof!" he said. "Come and help us!"

So the man *pulled* the turnip and the woman *pulled* the man and the little boy *pulled* the woman and the little girl *pulled* the little boy and the dog *pulled* the little girl and the cat *pulled* the dog. They *pulled* with all their might.

But they couldn't pull up the enormous turnip!

The cat spied a little mouse sitting under a cabbage leaf. "Miaow!" she called. "Come and help us!"

So the man *pulled* the turnip and the woman *pulled* the man and the little boy *pulled* the woman and the little girl *pulled* the little boy and the dog *pulled* the little girl and the cat *pulled* the dog and the little mouse *pulled* the cat.

They *pulled*…

    and *pulled*…

        with all their might.

"Don't… stop!" panted the man.
"I think… yes, I think… we've
done it!"

And at that the turnip came flying
out of the ground. The cat fell on
top of the little mouse and the
dog fell on top of the cat and the
little girl fell on top of the dog
and the little boy fell on top of the
little girl and the man fell on top
of the woman and what fell on top
of the man?

The most enormous turnip
anyone had ever seen!

When everyone had finished
laughing they picked themselves
up.

"You must stay and have dinner
with us," said the man and his
wife to the little boy and the little
girl and the dog and the cat and
the little mouse.

The turnip was *DELICIOUS!*
And you know, it was *so*
enormous that they haven't
finished eating it yet!

The Three Billy Goats Gruff

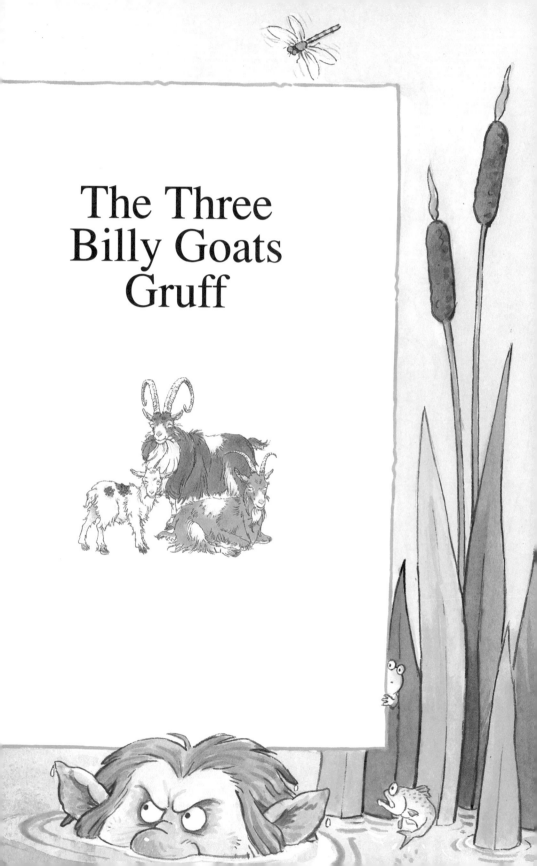

Once upon a time there were three billy goats called Gruff. One day, they set off in search of some sweet, green grass.

Very soon the goats came to a river. Across the river there was a meadow, and in the meadow grew the finest grass that any of them had ever seen.

Now, there was a wooden bridge over the river, and under this bridge lived a *very* fierce and ugly troll. Every time he heard footsteps going *trip, trap, trip, trap,* across the bridge, he jumped out and gobbled up whoever was trying to cross.

The three billy goats Gruff were very frightened of the troll, but they still longed to eat the sweet, green grass.

After a while the youngest billy goat Gruff stepped forward. "I'm tired of waiting," he said. "I will try to cross the bridge."

Trip, trap, trip, trap, went the little goat's hooves on the wooden planks. Soon he was halfway across.

Suddenly, *up* popped the ugly troll! "Who's that trip-trapping over *my* bridge?" he roared.

"It's only me… the littlest billy goat Gruff," said the frightened goat in a tiny voice. "I'm off to the meadow to eat the green grass."

"Then I'm coming to gobble you up!" roared the troll.

"Oh, *please* don't gobble me up," said the youngest billy goat Gruff. "Wait until the second billy goat Gruff comes along. He's much fatter than I am."

And the youngest billy goat Gruff crossed the bridge and skipped off into the meadow to eat the sweet, green grass.

Then the second billy goat Gruff stepped forward. "Now I will try to cross the bridge," he said.

Trip, trap, trip, trap, went his hooves on the wooden planks. Soon he was halfway across.

Suddenly, *up* popped the ugly troll! "Who's that trip-trapping over *my* bridge?" he roared.

"It's only me… the second billy goat Gruff," said the goat. "I'm off to the meadow to eat the green grass."

"Then I'm going to gobble you up!" roared the troll.

"Oh, *please* don't gobble me up," said the second billy goat Gruff. "Wait until the third billy goat Gruff comes along. He's *very* big and fat!"

And the second billy goat Gruff crossed the bridge and skipped off into the meadow to eat the sweet, green grass.

At last the biggest billy goat Gruff
decided to cross the bridge.

*Trip, trap, trip, trap, bang, bang,
bang, bang!* went his hooves on
the wooden planks, until he was
halfway across the bridge.

Suddenly, *up* popped the ugly troll!

"Who's that trip-trapping over *my* bridge?" roared the troll.

"It's me… the biggest billy goat Gruff," said the goat in his loud, gruff voice. "I'm off to the meadow to eat the green grass."

"Then I'm coming to gobble you up!" roared the troll.

"Oh no, you're not!" bellowed the biggest billy goat Gruff. "I'M COMING TO GOBBLE *YOU* UP!"

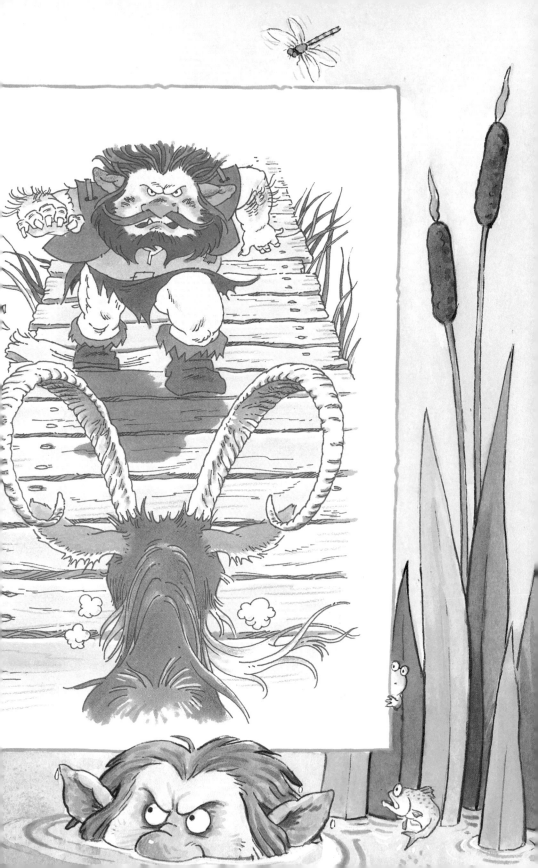

Then the biggest billy goat Gruff lowered his mighty horns and thundered towards the troll. *Trip, trap, trip, trap, bang, bang, BANG, BANG!*

He butted the ugly troll high into the air.

SPLASH! The troll fell down and down, head first into the deep water. The river rushed on, carrying the troll far, far away.

The biggest billy goat Gruff smiled to himself and skipped off into the meadow to eat the sweet, green grass.

The ugly troll was never seen again. And from that day on, no one was afraid to cross the bridge.

As for the three billy goats Gruff, they all ate so much sweet, green grass that they grew into very fat billy goats indeed!

The Little Red Hen

Once upon a time there was a little red hen who lived on a farm.

One morning, the little red hen found some grains of wheat. She took them to her friends in the farmyard.

"Who will help me to plant this wheat?" the little red hen asked her friends.

"Not I," said the cat.

"Not I," said the rat.

"Not I," said the pig.

"Then I shall plant the wheat myself,"
said the little red hen.

And that's just what she did. She
planted the grains in a neat row in the
sunniest part of the field.

The little red hen looked after the wheat carefully. She watered it and watched it grow.

At last the wheat was tall and strong and golden. The little red hen knew it was ready to be cut.

"Who will help me to cut the wheat?"
the little red hen asked her friends.

"Not I," said the cat.

"Not I," said the rat.

"Not I," said the pig.

"Then I shall cut the wheat myself," said the little red hen.

And that's just what she did. With her little scythe, she carefully cut down each stalk of golden wheat.

Then she went back to her friends.
"Who will help me to take
the wheat to the miller?"
she asked.

"Not I," said the cat.

"Not I," said the rat.

"Not I," said the pig.

"Then I shall take the wheat to the miller myself," said the little red hen.

And that's just what she did. She carried the wheat to the mill, and the miller ground it into flour. He put the flour into a sack for the little red hen.

The little red hen took the sack of flour back to the farmyard.

"Who will help me to take this flour to the baker?" she asked her friends.

"Not I," said the cat.

"Not I," said the rat.

"Not I," said the pig.

"Then I shall take it to the baker myself," said the little red hen.

And that's just what she did. The baker made the flour into a loaf of fresh, tasty bread. The little red hen took it back to the farmyard.

"Who will help me to eat this bread?" the little red hen asked her friends.

"I will!" said the cat.

"I will!" said the rat.

"I will!" said the pig.

"No, you will not!" said the little red hen. "I shall eat this fresh, tasty bread all by myself!"

And that's just what she did!

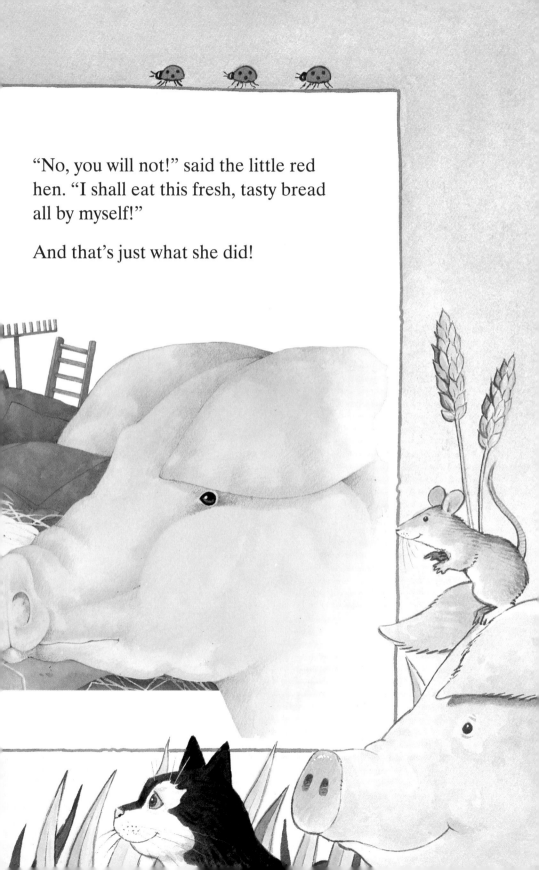